For my grandson Virgil.

 FriesenPress

One Printers Way
Altona, MB R0G 0B0
Canada

www.friesenpress.com

ISBN
978-1-03-913702-8 (Hardcover)
978-1-03-913701-1 (Paperback)
978-1-03-913703-5 (eBook)

1. JUVENILE FICTION, STORIES IN VERSE

Distributed to the trade by The Ingram Book Company

Lumpy Snow
and
Frosty Hats

WRITTEN AND ILLUSTRATED BY
GERRY KERYLUIK

Snow is falling and it might get deep,
I should shovel some before I sleep.

I could sweep up the snow at my feet,
And shovel a path out to the street.

I will do this to help my dad.
It will make him very glad.

This should be a lot of fun,
And be very tidy when I am done.

Into Dad's shop to find my tools,
I'll finish this task before night cools.

A broom and **shovel** are good to choose.
These are the tools for me to use.

An axe, a saw, and a
hammer I found.
What is that, there
on the ground?

There's a broom, a rake,
and there's a spade,

But no **shovel** with
red handle and blade.

Is it in the garage
near my bike,
Hanging on the wall
from a big spike?

I see two helmets and a spotted green hat,
A blue coat, a ball, and even a bat.

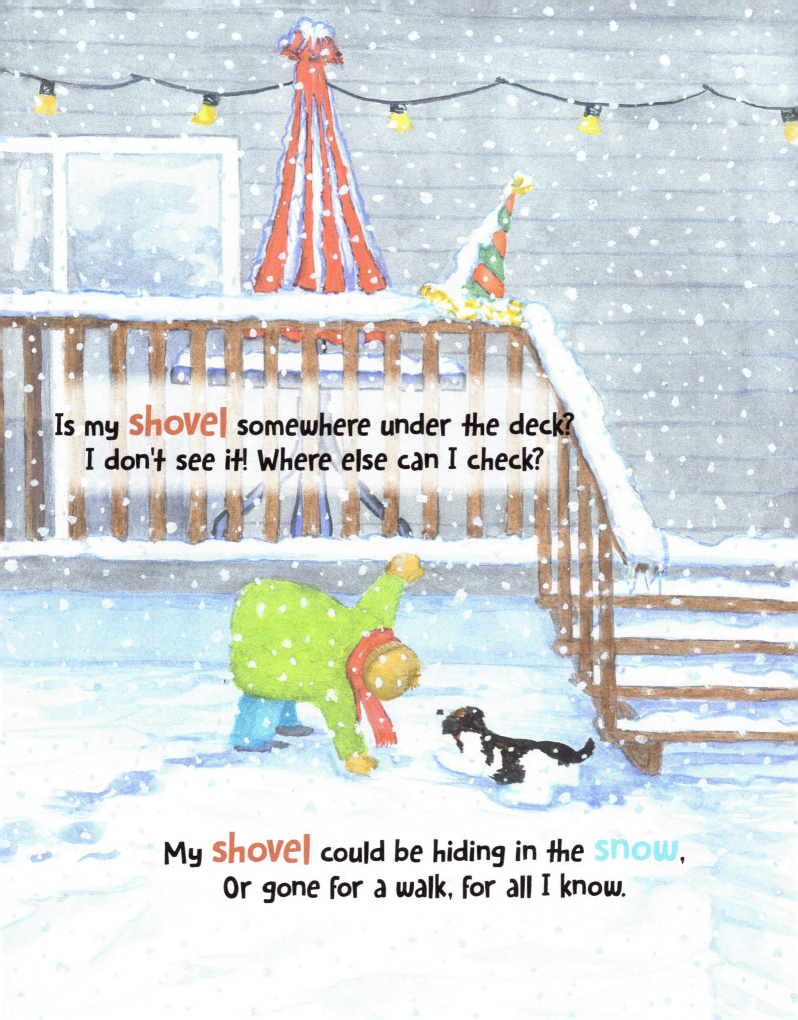

Is my **shovel** somewhere under the deck?
I don't see it! Where else can I check?

My **shovel** could be hiding in the **snow**,
Or gone for a walk, for all I know.

I spy with my eye, a wee bit of red,
Hidden in the snow straight ahead.

Could it be my shovel in a snowy hump?
It certainly is a big snowy lump.

Jax is digging the snowy lump out.
We'll discover what this is about.

Oh my! Would you look at that!
It's a sombrero, a Mexican hat.

What is this beside the trash can?
Oh, it's my mom's old turkey pan,
And there are some turkey bones too.

But my red shovel
is nowhere in view.

Is my **shovel** behind the shed?
Maybe it's somewhere
under my bed.

I can't find it here in the **snow**,
So to my bedroom, I will go.

Up the steps and into my house,
I will be quiet as a little dormouse.

I will have a peek under my bed,
to find my shovel
that is red.

I hang my coat by the door,
Mittens and boots I leave on the floor.

I pull up my socks
nice and snug,
While I sit here on
the rug.

Oh my! this is a place
I should clean.
I see dust bunnies and
something green.

JAMIE'S ROOM

Yuck, a piece of toast and a sock.
there's the key for Grandma's clock.

Is my **shovel** in the closet?

No. But I found a **red rocket**,
And **yellow boots** for my feet.
My closet is tidy and quite neat.

Well, I just have to think.
Is my **shovel** by the sink?

Is it in the tub
with my duck?
If it were, it would
get stuck.

My **shovel** is hidden very well.
Where it hides I cannot tell.

Could it be somewhere in the hall?
Wow! Here's my new soccer ball.

Is my **red shovel** in the **blue** bin?
Hmmm! A smelly tin and a fish fin.

Kit Cat sees what I'm looking at,
And Mom says,
"Jamie, that's not for the cat."

Where might a red shovel go to hide? I will search some more outside.

Oh dear! Would you look at that! The wind blows a frozen black hat!

Put on a coat and boots for the storm.
A scarf and mittens will keep me warm.

Now I'm ready to search some more,
In places I did not search before.

Is my **shovel** near a beehive?
I wonder if bees are still alive?

Little chickadees are getting fed.
Hey, there's a tool, and it is **red**.

What is over there, in the tree?
Is it my **shovel** waiting from me?

It's a squirrel and there's a hat.
I have a hat, just like that.

Holy moly! It's getting too late.
Is my **shovel** by the gate?

Here's a stick just
like a wand.
Is my **red shovel**
near the pond?

I see three fish
under the ice,
And two raccoons
trying to be nice.

I'll stay away and won't go near.
My red shovel wouldn't be here.

Snowflakes are falling on my face.
My shovel is in some other place.

I will lie down here in the snow,
And make a snow angel before I go.

The light by the door
is shining bright.
And very soon it
will be night.

My mom would want me home by now.
Do I hear Kit Cat's meow?

I looked and looked everywhere.
But did not peek under the stair.

A Christmas tree and Santa's red hat,
And here are bobbles for Kit Cat.

Is my **red shovel** behind this door?
There is stuff all over the floor.

Boxes of books, and a hat with strings,
Cards and comics, photos and things.

It is very good to search and look, I just found my favourite book.

Reading books makes me smile. I'll go upstairs and read a while.

I searched a lot and did my best.
Now it's time to read and rest.

JAMIE'S ROOM

Kit Cat and I will
have a cuddle,

And tomorrow,
I will find my red shovel.

Guided Questions

Jamie is done searching for today. Do you remember what Jamie was looking for?

What tools did Jamie find?
What tools did you discover?

What did Jamie find under the bed? What could you discover under your bed?

What animals did Jamie see?
What other animals did you notice?
Do you have a favourite animal or pet?

What toys did Jamie find?
What other toys did you notice?
What is your favourite toy?

Where did Jamie search and
look outside?
Where did Jamie search and look
inside the house?
Where could Jamie search and
look for a snow shovel tomorrow?

Do you have a snow shovel?
Where would you find a snow shovel?
Why do you think Jamie could not find
a snow shovel?

What would be a different ending for
this story?
What does this story remind you of?
What jobs do you do to help your family?

How many hats did Jamie find?
How many hats did you discover?

Do you have a favourite hat?
Could you draw your favourite hat?

CPSIA information can be obtained
at www.ICGtesting.com
Printed in the USA
BVHW022310120622
639369BV00001B/3